By Mary Man-Kong
Based on the original screenplay by Elise Allen
Illustrated by Ulkutay Design Group and Pat Pakula

Special thanks to Vicki Jaeger, Monica Okazaki, Kathleen Warner, Emily Kelly, Christine Chang,
Tanya Mann, Rob Hudnut, Tiffany J. Shuttleworth, Walter P. Martishius, Luke Carroll, Lil Reichmann,
Pam Prostarr, David Lee, Anita Lee, Andrea Schimpl, Tulin Ulkutay, and Ayse Ulkutay

 A GOLDEN BOOK • NEW YORK

Published in the United States by Golden Books, an imprint of Random House Children's Books, a division of Random
House, Inc., 1745 Broadway, New York, NY 10019, and in Canada by Random House of Canada Limited, Toronto. No part of
this book may be reproduced or copied in any form without permission from the copyright owner. Golden Books, A Golden
Book, A Little Golden Book, the G colophon, and the distinctive gold spine are registered trademarks of Random House, Inc.
www.randomhouse.com/kids
Educators and librarians, for a variety of teaching tools, visit us at www.randomhouse.com/teachers
Library of Congress Control Number: 2009904822   ISBN: 978-0-375-85733-1
Printed in the United States of America   10 9 8 7 6 5 4 3 2 1

"She's the queen of the waves!" the crowd cheered from the shore.

Merliah Summers waved to her friends as she rode her surfboard. Merliah had always loved the water, and now she was competing in Malibu Beach High School's surfing competition.

"Life is perfect!" Merliah thought.

Then Merliah noticed her hair—it was *turning pink*!
Shocked by the change, she dove off her surfboard.
As she examined her strange new hair color, Merliah
suddenly realized that she was *breathing underwater*!

Just then, someone called her name. It was a beautiful
pink, sparkly dolphin! "My name is Zuma," the dolphin
said. Merliah couldn't believe it. But there were more
surprises in store for the young surfer. . . .

As they swam toward a cove, Zuma revealed that Merliah was the daughter of Calissa, the mermaid queen of an underwater kingdom called Oceana. Long ago, Calissa's wicked sister, Eris, had taken over Oceana. To protect her daughter, Calissa had given Merliah a special shell necklace and sent her to live with her human grandfather in Malibu.

Merliah didn't want to believe she
was half mermaid! She ripped off her
necklace and smashed it against the
rocks. Suddenly, Merliah saw a vision
of her mother being held prisoner.

"You need to return to Oceana to free your mother and defeat Eris, just as the Destinies have predicted," Zuma told Merliah.

"Maybe my mother can help me get my normal life back," the young surfer thought.

The dolphin led Merliah down to Oceana—the most amazing place she had ever seen!

"Eris mustn't hear that there's a human in town," said Zuma. "We need to get you a tail."

The dolphin brought Merliah to a clothing boutique that belonged to two mermaids named Xylie and Kayla. They quickly created a beautiful fake tail.

Snouts, their playful pet sea lion, barked his approval.

Unfortunately, Eris had already discovered that Merliah was in Oceana. So the evil mermaid snuck down to the secret dungeon where she kept Calissa locked away.

"Tell me where she is, Sister!" Eris demanded.

"I don't know what you're talking about," Calissa replied. She hoped her daughter, Merliah, was safe.

Meanwhile, Merliah and her new friends swam to the Destinies for guidance. They told Merliah that to defeat Eris, she would need to find the Celestial Comb, a dreamfish, and Eris's protective necklace.

The Celestial Comb was hidden in the Yafos Caves. No merfolk could climb the sparkling rock wall to get the Celestial Comb. But Merliah had legs! She quickly scaled the wall and grabbed the comb. "I've got it!" she cried triumphantly.

Next, Merliah had to find a dreamfish in the Andenato Current. The current was very strong, and no one could swim through it. But Merliah knew she could *surf* through it on a giant shell!

The dreamfish were very impressed with Merliah's surfing. One young dreamfish promised to grant a wish for her. "Call when you need me, and I will come," he said.

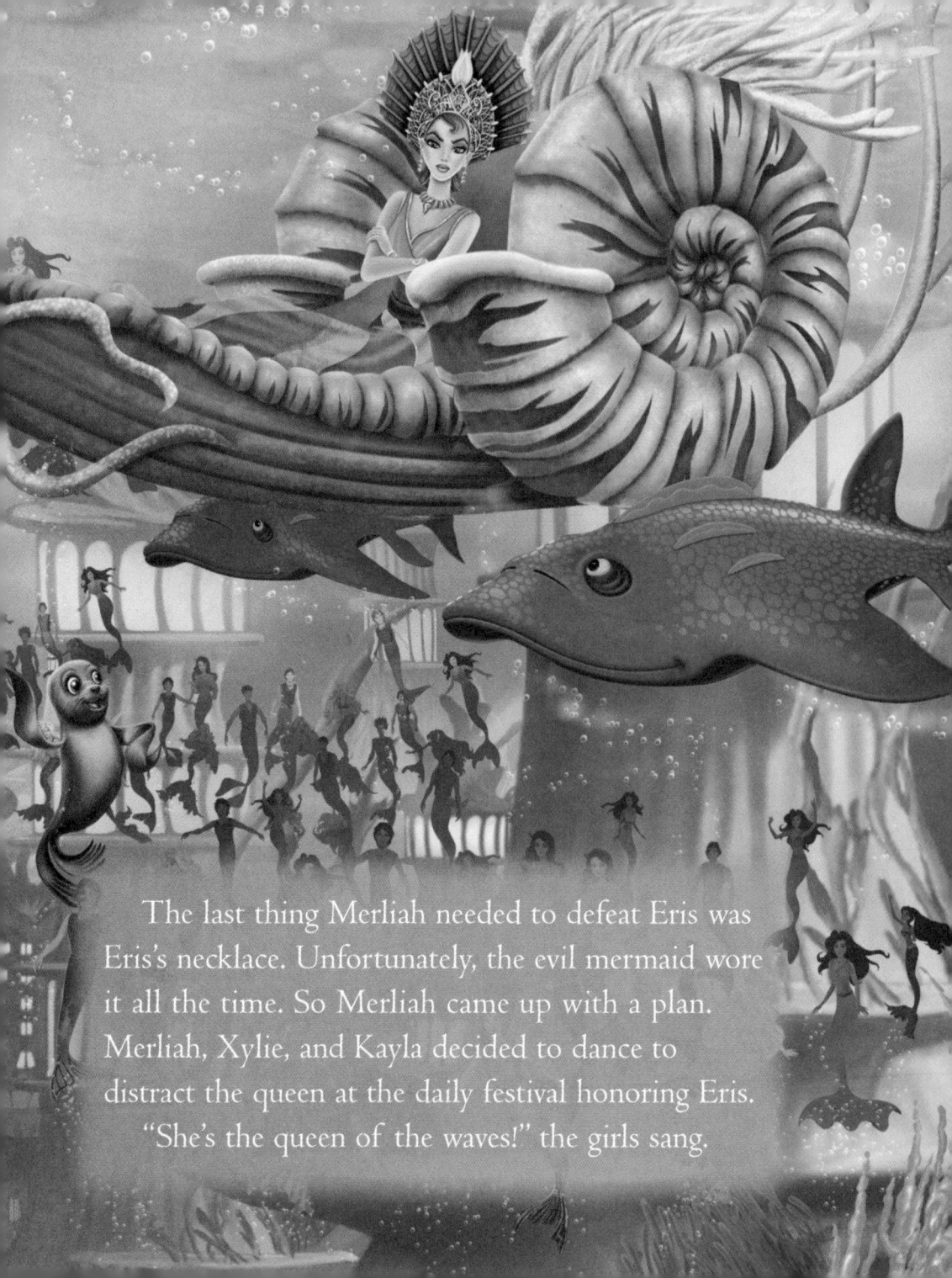

The last thing Merliah needed to defeat Eris was Eris's necklace. Unfortunately, the evil mermaid wore it all the time. So Merliah came up with a plan. Merliah, Xylie, and Kayla decided to dance to distract the queen at the daily festival honoring Eris. "She's the queen of the waves!" the girls sang.

While Eris was enjoying the show, Merliah saw her chance—and snatched the necklace!

The evil mermaid ordered her manta shark guards to capture Merliah. When they rushed after her, the manta sharks tore Merliah's fake tail.

"You!" Eris cried. Realizing that Merliah was Calissa's daughter, Eris quickly trapped her in a churning whirlpool.

As Merliah swirled helplessly in the whirlpool, she
called to the little dreamfish. He magically appeared
and offered to return her to Malibu. Merliah was
tempted to accept and go back to her old life. But
her mother and Oceana still needed her help, so
she decided to stay.

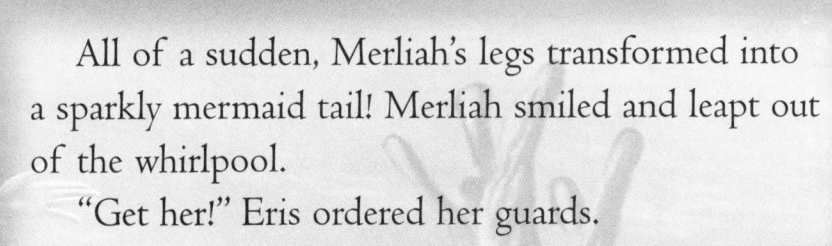

All of a sudden, Merliah's legs transformed into a sparkly mermaid tail! Merliah smiled and leapt out of the whirlpool.

"Get her!" Eris ordered her guards.

"Wait!" Merliah cried. "You don't have to listen to her. I am the rightful heir to the throne. I have the Celestial Comb!"

Furious, Eris tried to push Merliah back into the whirlpool. But Merliah swam out of the way just in time. Eris was sucked into the swirling water—and transported to the deepest, darkest trench!

"Hooray!" the crowd shouted. Oceana was saved!

Calissa was freed from the dungeon and became queen again. She hugged Merliah and placed a new magical shell necklace around her daughter's neck.

"When you wish on it, you can control what you look like," Calissa explained. "Then you can move easily between the human and the mermaid world."

Back in Malibu, Merliah rode a monster wave
with her friends. She smiled, knowing her underwater
family was cheering for her, too. Merliah had a home
in both worlds—and life was perfect!